Don't Forget the Oatmeal!

A Supermarket Word Book

Featuring Jim Henson's
Sesame Street Muppets

by B. G. Ford
Illustrated by
Jean Chandler

A SESAME STREET/GOLDEN PRESS BOOK
Published by Western Publishing Company, Inc.
in conjunction with Children's Television Workshop.

©1980 Children's Television Workshop. Muppet characters
©1980 Muppets, Inc. All rights reserved. Printed in U.S.A.
SESAME STREET®, the SESAME STREET SIGN, and SESAME STREET BOOK CLUB
are trademarks and service marks of Children's Television Workshop.
GOLDEN® and GOLDEN PRESS® are trademarks of Western Publishing Company, Inc.
No part of this book may be reproduced or copied in any form without
written permission from the publisher.
Library of Congress Catalog Card Number: 80-80340
ISBN 0-307-23109-7

butter

cheese

flour sugar soap

salt

knife

cutting board

refrigerator

APPLES
ORANGES
MILK
EGGS
PAPER NAPKINS
SOAP
PEAS
PEANUT
BUTTER
HAMBURGER
MEAT
PICKLES
BREAD

garbage can

One morning Ernie and Bert were getting ready to go to
the supermarket. Ernie was checking the shopping list to
make sure he had written down everything they needed.

"Let's see," he said. "Apples, oranges, milk, eggs, paper
napkins, soap, peas, peanut butter, hamburger meat, pickles,
and bread. Is that all, Bert?"

bowl

pots

cabinet

mixing spoons

sponge

pot holders

tea kettle

sink

stove

string

scissors

"You forgot to write down oatmeal, Ernie," said Bert. "You know I like to have a bowl of delicious, nutritious oatmeal every morning."

"Don't worry, Bert, we won't forget it," said Ernie, as he picked up his piggy bank and hurried out the door.

At the fruit stand outside the supermarket Bert weighed the apples on a scale while Ernie got the oranges.

"Why do you have that string tied around your finger, Bert?" asked Ernie.

"To help me remember the oatmeal," said Bert.

Just then along came Cookie Monster.

"Cookies on sale today," he said, pointing to a large sign. "Me buy lots and lots of cookies. Me buy enough cookies to last all year!"

plums

blueberries

strawberries

watermelon

lemons

cherries

oranges

Inside the market, Ernie and Bert began to gather the rest of the things on their list.

"We need milk and eggs from the dairy counter," said Ernie.

"What about the oatmeal, Ernie?" said Bert.

"Later, Bert, later," said Ernie as he hurried to get the milk and eggs.

DAIRY PRODUCTS

cream

margarine

milk

eggs

butter

ice cream

APPLES ✓
ORANGES ✓
MILK
EGGS
PAPER NAPKINS
SOAP
PEAS
PEANUT
BUTTER
HAMBURGER
MEAT
PICKLES
BREAD

Ernie came running back to the wagon. "Look what I found, Bert, old buddy! I got some terrific Cheesie Pleasie, and here's some delicious Ice Cream Supreme!"

"But we just need milk and eggs!" said Bert, looking at the shopping list. "You'll have to put those other things back."

At the end of the dairy aisle, Cookie Monster was putting some cartons of milk in his cart. "Mmmm!" he said. "Me love milk with cookies!"

paper plates

dish detergent

sandwich bags

paper cups

plastic wrap

laundry soap

straws

bath soap

trash bags

aluminum foil

Bert pushed the cart into the next aisle to look for
paper napkins and soap. Suddenly Ernie came running up
behind him with his arms full.

SOAPS
PAPER PRODUCTS

paper towels

paper napkins

toilet paper

soap pads

RUB·A·DUB   RUB·A·DUB   RUB·A·DUB

floor wax

ZOO   ZOO   ZO

mops

APPLES
ORANGES
MILK
EGGS
PAPER NAPKINS
SOAP
PEAS
PEANUT
BUTTER
HAMBURGER
MEAT
PICKLES
BREAD

"Wait just a minute, Ernie!" said Bert. "We don't need
paper plates and cups today! We don't need sandwich bags
and straws! We need only napkins and soap...and *oatmeal*!
You'll just have to put those other things back!"

While Ernie put back the things they didn't need, Bert went along to the next aisle to get the peas and peanut butter.

"Why don't you buy some vegetables, Cookie?" said Bert as he weighed the peas. "Vegetables are good for you."

Cookie ate a handful of peas. "Mmmm! Peas not bad. Me like peas!" he said.

"Good," said Bert. "Don't forget to pay for them."

ham

salami

chicken

steak

lamb chops

frankfurters

sausages   bologna

liverwurst

bacon

Ernie stopped at the meat counter.
"One pound of hamburger meat, please," he said
to the butcher.
"Here you are!" said the butcher.

After getting pickles at the delicatessen counter, Bert checked the shopping list. Then he noticed the string tied around his finger.

"I mustn't forget the oatmeal," he said.

"Did you say OATMEAL?" asked Cookie Monster, running down the aisle. "Me *love* oatmeal cookies! Where they hide cookies in this supermarket, anyway?"

"Why don't you try the next aisle?" asked Bert.

biscuits

crackers

cookies

bread

rolls

pies

cake mix

rice puffs

puffed corn

corn flakes

shredded wheat

BAKERY-CEREALS

OATMEAL

Cookie Monster looked
into the next aisle....
"COOKIES!!" he shouted.

"Yummy!" cried Cookie Monster, running toward the shelves and grabbing a bag of cookies.
"Here oatmeal cookies!"

"And peanut butter cookies! Goody!"

"Coconut macaroons! Delicious!"

"Marshmallow cookies!
Oh, gimme lots of these!"

"And Mint Chipparoos!"

"And chocolate fudge creams!"

By the time Ernie and Bert reached the bakery
aisle, they found Cookie Monster on the floor,
surrounded by bags and boxes of cookies.
   "We'd better help Cookie clean up this mess,"
said Ernie.

"He doesn't need all these cookies," said Bert, picking up a box of Mint Chipparoos.

Ernie and Bert helped Cookie Monster put things back where they belonged and reminded him to pay for the cookies he had broken and eaten. They left just one bag of cookies in his cart.

books

cash register

Finally Ernie and Bert pushed their cart up to the checkout counter to pay for their groceries.

"Gee, Ernie, I thought we'd never finish our shopping."

"It's a good thing I brought my piggy bank along, Bert," said Ernie. "We have just enough money for everything."

cashier

paper bag

checkout counter

magazines

Ernie and Bert hurried along Sesame Street, carrying their bags of groceries.

Cookie Monster headed straight home for his afternoon snack of cookies and milk.

Back home in their kitchen, Ernie and Bert took the groceries out of the bags. Bert put the jars in the cabinets and Ernie put the milk and eggs in the refrigerator.

Bert read the shopping list again: "Apples, oranges, milk, eggs, paper napkins, soap, peas, peanut butter, hamburger meat, pickles, and bread...."

"OH, NO!" Bert groaned, collapsing into a chair.
"What's the matter, Bert, old buddy?" asked Ernie.

Bert held up the finger that still had a string tied around it.
"We forgot to buy the OATMEAL!"

ABCDEFGHIJKL